Alice Brown

The Road to Castaly

Alice Brown

The Road to Castaly

ISBN/EAN: 9783743303393

Manufactured in Europe, USA, Canada, Australia, Japa

Cover: Foto ©Andreas Hilbeck / pixelio.de

Manufactured and distributed by brebook publishing software
(www.brebook.com)

Alice Brown

The Road to Castaly

THE
ROAD TO CASTALY

ALICE BROWN

BOSTON
COPELAND AND DAY
MDCCCXCVI

TO

LOUISE IMOGEN GUINEY

THE ROAD TO CASTALY

SOVEREIGNS of the sacred mount,
Circled round her silver fount, —
Sires of life who song began, —
Swiftest heralds, ye who ran
With winged sandals up the way
Where unled the Muses stray :
Hear us ! we who haste to ye,
Pensioners of poesy.
Native airs of song ye breathe ;
Deathless buds your foreheads wreathe ;
Yet not wholly are ye blest
Over us, who walk confest
Beggars of the charity
Shuttled 'twixt the earth and sky ;
Destined aye to keep the road
Far from that august abode ;
Fated ne'er to taste the spring
Set for poet's quickening.
Only born to braid our lays
In the garlanding of praise ;
Born to praise the Muses Nine,
Praise the One unknown, divine,

Who upon our bosoms set
His unfading amulet :
" Ever seek and never see;
Die uncrowned yet votary."
Fain are we of beechen boughs ;
We are they the pine endows
With hot scent of pungent power,
Sealing so the noonday hour.
Bitter bread to us is sweet.
Highway brambles kiss our feet.
Dust yclad, our dreams we sing
Round about the roadside spring.
Nay, not all unblest are we
Wayfarers to Castaly !

Contents

THE ROAD TO CASTALY	*Page*	vii
WOOD-LONGING		1
PAN		4
SUNRISE ON MANSFIELD MOUNTAIN		8
ESCAPE		10
CANDLEMAS		12
MARINERS		13
MORNING IN CAMP		15
RED MAGIC		18
MIST		19
WHEN DAYS ARE LONG		19
REVELATION		19
THE HEART AND LOVE		20
LIFE		22
PAGAN PRAYERS		22
YESTERDAY		22
NO ANSWER		23
AN INVOCATION		23
THE RETURN		24
FOREWARNED		26
A WEST-COUNTRY LOVER		27
DESTINY		29
LOVE DENIED		29
ON PILGRIMAGE		31

MAGDALEN	*Page* 32
A FAREWELL	32
TO CIRCE	33
RENEWAL	33
THE MESSAGE	34
FAMINE	36
ON THE FIELD	36
EDWIN BOOTH	37
HORA CHRISTI	40
IN EXTREMIS	42
KNIGHTHOOD ETERNAL	43
HEIMGEGANGEN	45
SLEEP	46
LETHE	47
THE SILENT WATCH	48
TRILBY	49
DREAMS	50
THE POET	52
THE SLANDERER	52
SEAWARD BOUND	53
TEWKESBURY ABBEY	55
CONTENT	55
THE HEART'S TRUE CHOICE	56
THE SPIRIT'S HOUR	56
MAN TO WOMAN	57
THE UNSEEN FELLOWSHIP	58
THE FLIGHT OF THE FAIRIES	60

WOOD–LONGING

O BOOKS, my books, ye give me naught for
all my asking!
Vain is the spirit's tasking
To raise up honor from the printed line,
Or scent ripe clusters in the long-dried wine
Of antique banquets spilled upon the page.
O books are but the cage
Where echoes of the spirit sing,
Nor ever truly ring .
The clarion cry, the tabor and the pipe,
Whereto, ere yet the year is ripe,
The happy rivers run, with rhythmic glancing,
And all the fauns and satyrs fall a-dancing!
One medicine hath life for sick and sane ;
One crown of joy, one solacing for pain.
Who beauty seeks and truth,
Or springs of vanished youth,
With fitful joyance, or that full content
For gods and lilies meant,

Swift be his passing to the field and wood,
To face the immemorial passion of the flood,
The amplitude of all the fertile plains,
Where mild abundance reigns ;
The seated majesty of crownèd hills,
Whose mantling shadow fills
The well-loved valley softly laid below,
Fed from the rock, in royal overflow.

Spirit, what wilt thou dare
Just to be one with earth and air ?
To read the writing on the river bed,
And trace God's mystical mosaic overhead ?
O sweet familiar of the rustling leaf,
Dear idle mourner of the gathered sheaf,
Lover and guardian of the beech-tree's bole,
Wooer unwearied of her dryad soul,
Tippler on sacramental wine,
The great round world is thine !
Thy rich inheritance to tread the earth
When all the ecstasy of myriad birth
Afflicts her with a rapturous shuddering ;
To feel the beating of the mighty wing
Wherewith the great wind winnows out her halls,
Where never footing falls
But it makes music, as the sweep of stars,
And not one jarring note the lyric heaven mars.
Thy happy destiny to lie
Within the thriftless grasses, opulently
Sifting thy jewels with an idle touch,
Still heedless of how little or how much

2

The careless giving of the royal hour,
For all the morn is thine, and the great sun
  thy dower.

O happy beggary !
O greedy eye
And all unsated heart !
Thou only hast a part
In treasures manifold
Of wealth that grows not old.
O incommunicable speech !
For he who reads a book may preach
A hundred sermons from its foolish rote
And rhyme reiterant on one dull note.
But he who spends an hour within the wood
Hath fed on fairy food ;
And who hath eaten of the forest fruit
Is ever mute.
Nothing may he reveal.
Nature hath set her seal
Of honor on anointed lips ;
And one who daring dips
His cup within her potent brew
Hath drunk of silence too.
What doth the robin say,
And what the martial jay ?
Who 'll swear the bluebird's lilt is all of love,
Or who translate the desolation of the dove ?
For even in the common speech
Of feathered fellows, each to each,
Abideth still the primal mystery,

Wood-Longing. The brooding past, the germ of life to be ;
And one poor weed, upspringing to the sun,
Breeds all creation's wonder, new begun.
Come, then, who would be free,
Break bonds and run with me !
Stay not your hasting till the mystic round
Of green, untrodden ground
Hath hid us from the eyes of men ;
There to be young again,
There to forget old passion's folly
And all dull learning's melancholy.
Come, for the forest calls !
Come, ere the echo falls !

PAN

HARK ! you may hear him stirring,
More softly than the whirring
Of filmy, hair-veined wings,
Or thrill of echoing strings
When the sad pine, with weaving minstrelsy,
Mocks the imagined music of the sea.
The fall of ebon hoof !
Stand lightly by, aloof,
And you may see him pass,
Unwounding the lush grass,
Dropping diffusive balm
From honey breath and careless hollowed palm,—
Known of the hawk, unnoted now of man,
The great god Pan !

4

Where was he hiding
When men, deriding
The lisping lore of years when years were young,
And song held some sweet measures yet unsung,
Declared him dead,
His great dominion fled,
And nailed their rhymes above his mossy bier?
Ah! in the youth or age o' the year,
In sunshine, or in midnight murk,
Still did the goat-god lurk
In the green forest glade,
Of naught afraid
But of the curious eye,
Of ominous crash, and echo-frighting cry :
"'This way he ran!
Surely the one called Pan!'"

In the deep wood!
The wood so deep that one scarce enters there
With willing foot, but warm-left lair
Of timorous beast is found,
And o'er the hollow ground
Faint, pattering paws of thrifty squirrels tread;
The sanctuary where spent winds are fled,
And nuts lie stored
Richer than Rhine-washed hoard;
Where every hollow tree hath honey cells;
Here where the wild dove dwells,
And one secluded, choir-remembering thrush
Strikes silvernly across the solemn hush
Of the vast shadowy stillness, with his flute

Pan.   And cymbals, — and is mute.
Where the shy partridge rounds her nest,
And by lone Silence blest,
Teaches her young the sweet wood-lessoning
Of hiding under leaf and flight on fluttering
    wing.
There, on a day of all delight,
Dropping through purpling reaches down to shore-
    less night,
Day sprung from some far, Titan-bosomed source,
And leaving, in its course,
The hills enriched, the valleys drowned with joy—
Day for a god's employ —
I saw him, I,
Unworthily
Spying upon him, creeping in the deep
Removèd courts, where Dian's self might sleep.
Over my crawling flesh swift prescience ran :
The living Pan !
His brow was crowned that day,
Not with the myrtle and the bay,
Or flower ambrosial sprung from storied fields,
But all the woodland yields
Of blessèd homely leaf
Garnered in Summer's sheaf
Of joys.   The wilding clematis
Roved o'er his regnant front with rioting kiss;
The royal goldenrod
There learned to nod,
Entreating she might touch his tangled hair,
And so transmute herself to fairest fair ;

6

Great lilies lustred o'er the living crown ;
And trailing down
His mighty sides, the dull hop-vine
Did with her dreaming mates entwine.
Upon one shaggy knee
He handled tenderly
A youngling fox, whose mother stood thereby,
Watching with worshipful and drowsy eye
The laughing god and laughing little one,
Both children of the sun,
Loved of the wind,
And understood by all four-footed kind.
Ah ! who but one reed-piping in the wood might
    now
Sing of the god himself, his music-haunted brow,
His cheeks, like autumn hillocks, overspread
With bloom of russet red
Richer than wine spilled o'er young maple tips ?
His glowing lips
For generous laughter curved ; the all-compelling
    eye
Where buried sunlit sands discovered lie ———·

    .   .   .   .   .

But hush ! ah, hush ! lay listening ear
To earth !   Dost thou not hear
His rhythmic tread ?   The gladdened air
Drips with the wood-scent from his tossing hair ;
The very cloud
Trails lower ; and the oriole's loud
Bright plaint is piercing, unsubdued,
The lattice of her leaf-wrought solitude ;

Pan.   The robin blither sings,
The blindworm dreams of wings.
Lower! bow low! abase thy trivial state, O man!
He comes, the earth-god, Pan!

SUNRISE ON MANSFIELD MOUNTAIN

O SWIFT forerunners, rosy with the race!
    Spirits of dawn, divinely manifest
Behind your blushing banners in the sky,
Daring invaders of Night's tenting-ground, —
How do ye strain on forward-bending foot,
Each to be first in heralding of joy!

With silence sandalled, so they weave their way,
And so they stand, with silence panoplied,
Chanting, through mystic symbollings of flame,
Their solemn invocation to the light.

O changeless guardians! O ye wizard firs!
What strenuous philter feeds your potency,
That thus ye rest, in sweet wood-hardiness,
Ready to learn of all and utter naught?
What breath may move ye, or what breeze invite
To odorous hot lendings of the heart?
What wind — but all the winds are yet afar,
And e'en the little tricksy zephyr sprites,
That fleet before them, like their elfin locks,

Have lagged in sleep, nor stir nor waken yet
To pluck the robe of patient majesty.

Too still for dreaming, too divine for sleep,
So range the firs, the constant, fearless ones.
Warders of mountain secrets, there they wait,
Each with his cloak about him, breathless, calm,
And yet expectant, as who knows the dawn,
And all night thrills with memory and desire,
Searching in what has been for what shall be :
The marvel of the ne'er familiar day,
Sacred investiture of life renewed,
The chrism of dew, the coronal of flame.
Low in the valley lies the conquered rout
Of man's poor, trivial turmoil, lost and drowned
Under the mist, in gleaming rivers rolled,
Where oozy marsh contends with frothing main.
And rounding all, springs one full, ambient arch,
One great good limpid world — so still, so still !
For no sound echoes from its crystal curve
Save four clear notes, the song of that lone bird
Who, brave but trembling, tries his morning hymn,
And has no heart to finish, for the awe
And wonder of this pearling globe of dawn.

Light, light eternal ! veiling-place of stars !
Light, the revealer of dread beauty's face !
Weaving whereof the hills are lambent clad !
Mighty libation to the Unknown God !
Cup whereat pine-trees slake their giant thirst
And little leaves drink sweet delirium !

9

Sunrise on Mansfield Mountain. Being and breath and potion! living soul
And all-informing heart of all that lives!
How can we magnify thine awful name
Save by its chanting: Light! and light! and light!
An exhalation from far sky retreats,
It grows in silence, as 't were self-create,
Suffusing all the dusky web of night.
But one lone corner it invades not yet,
Where low above a black and rimy crag
Hangs the old moon, thin as a battered shield,
The holy, useless shield of long-past wars,
Dinted and frosty, on the crystal dark.

But lo! the east, — let none forget the east,
Pathway ordained of old where He should tread.
Through some sweet magic common in the skies,
The rosy banners are with saffron tinct;
The saffron grows to gold, the gold is fire,
And led by silence more majestical
Than clash of conquering arms, He comes!   He
     comes!
He holds his spear benignant, sceptrewise,
And strikes out flame from the adoring hills.

ESCAPE

O MY people, my own Little People, come
     back
From your home in the house of dreams!
Build of your magic a shining track;
Set silver sails on the hurrying streams

10

That run from the rifts of the past !
Tie Jack-with-his-lantern on every mast,
To sing, " Good cheer,
Little mariner !
Here 's a tricksy defiance to every gale,
And a health to the billows whereon we sail!"
Pour from the flowers and out of the flood ;
From the hollows of moss in the heart of the
    wood !
Flitting and skipping, oh, leap and dance !
Warily trip it where fireflies glance !
O, hurry, I pray ye, nor waste ye
One moment, but hitherward haste ye !
Come, blink at this market of groans and sighs,
With elfin grimaces and wondering eyes ;
And drown all our chaffer of hatred and dole
With sweet limpid laughter that tickles the soul !
For the courage of manhood is dying,
And hearts are made only for sighing.
We 're sick for the sight of ye,
Starved for the sound of ye,
Faint for the lack of ye !
Sick for the sight of a coat of green,
A-shimmer like leaves in their morning sheen ;
Starved for the sound of a patter and play
Like iris drops on an April day !
For, O Little People ! our souls live alone,
Together, yet lone, in dwellings of stone.
And the corners are square, and the stone in
    blocks,
And there 's never the look of the lichened rocks ;

Escape. And we sit on benches of carven wood.
Now you know, Little People, it's never good
For a poor, poor soul to be pent in a place
Where the sky's a window and not a space ;
Nor to strive to be keeping its pinions free
When it never can nest in a living tree.
So come, little brothers, and laugh and sing;
Draw on the pavement a fairy ring !
Pull us into it, every one,
And set us dancing till day is done !
Then draw us dancing out of the town
Into the land where the sun goes down
Under the pennons that flame and fly
In a golden dream on a golden sky !

And there — but what happens is past all guess-
ing,
Past all thinking and all expressing.
Enough for the earth-worn soul to be
In a world where a man and a fay are free.

CANDLEMAS

O HEARKEN, all ye little weeds
That lie beneath the snow,
(So low, dear hearts, in poverty so low !)
The sun hath risen for royal deeds,
A valiant wind the vanguard leads ;
Now quicken ye, lest unborn seeds
Before ye rise and blow.

O furry living things, adream

Candle-mas.

O furry living things, adream
 On winter's drowsy breast,
(How rest ye there, how softly, safely rest!)
 Arise and follow where a gleam
 Of wizard gold unbinds the stream,
 And all the woodland windings seem
  With sweet expectance blest.

 My birds, come back! the hollow sky
  Is weary for your note.
(Sweet-throat, come back! O liquid, mellow
 throat!)
 Ere May's soft minions hereward fly,
 Shame on ye, laggards, to deny
 The brooding breast, the sun-bright eye,
  The tawny, shining coat!

MARINERS

WE are the warders of the middle world,
 Where ripples breathe with blossomy edges
 curled,
Like frostwork over lambent emeralds set,
Or changeful light from beauty's coronet.
Full-sailed, high-hearted, o'er the glassy brink
Of watery ways we slip and glide amain,
Into smooth hollows, rising link on link,
O'er toppling crests, down-dropping to the plain;
While our uncertain foothold still doth range
Through sweet and mystic fantasies of change.

13

Mariners. O beauty's lover! hither run, and roam
From ridge to ridge of unconstrainèd flight,
Where break the liquid shards about our keel,
Only to close again in serried light:
As passionate sunbeams rise and turn and wheel
And fix in keen array their javelins bright.
Here is assuaging of that ancient thirst
Begot by feeding on remembered days:
An image fair for hunger's empty gaze.
Lucent lagoons lie here berimmed with foam;
And inland eyes that loved a river first
Through the salt plash see threading silver gleam,
And touch the tress of Arethusa's stream.
Here when the mist her flimsy portal locks,
The unwearied vision wakes, to build a dream
Of trembling ferns and hoary-bearded rocks,
Of idling bushes by the runnel's bound,
And reaching trees in some fair orchard ground.

Through the green darkness of this watery life,
The hollow caverns of the under-sea,
Gigantic branches twine in waving strife,
And uncouth monsters wallow formlessly.
They know not us, nor guess the way we go.
Fill full the sail, O master wind, and blow!
Draw thou our homesick eyes, the while we flee,
To some sky solitude where dwells a star,
And points us where our heavenly fortunes are.

MORNING IN CAMP

VOUCHSAFE me now the holy cup of song,
  Ye to whom sacred chalices belong,
Attendant ministers of day and night!
The mystic golden cup, o'erchased with light,
And fine from foot to curve of carven brim;
For I would fill it to the circling rim
With those clear drops of heaven's ecstasy
Oozing like precious nard from beauty's tree:
Joy of the growing leaf, the bird, the wind,
Born to sink soundless into blood and mind,
To pierce the very heart of passion's core,
And so make one with being evermore.
Yea, niggard of the over-blossomed hour,
I would seal up its bliss-engendering power,
Caught in the miracle of rhythmic sound
As seeds are prisoned in their guardian ground,
And hold it for some day of dearth and pain,
That I might thus inherit wood and plain,
And of the weft of life make fantasy,
And revellings from out my poverty.

Awake at dawn! yet still with sleep endued,
But conscious of my tent's white solitude;
The strident cawing of the black-coat choir,
Dulcet in dissonance, untuned to lyre
As to the reed: a rasp of vibrant song
Wherein no note is well, but none falls wrong.
Keyed at wild will, but ever yet in tune,
Chimes the true chorus called by quiring June,

As though the unseen steeples of the air
Should rock with bliss, and that fine hidden stair
Whereby the heart climbs up to kiss her dream,
Bloom out resplendent in a rainbow gleam.
And faint, far notes like nestlings strive and spring,
Too little yet to trust their trembling wing.
These be the tiny feathered citizens
For whom the wood creates her airy glens,
And the great tolerant pine-tree waxeth high,
To give them covert from the love-bright sky.
These be our little brothers, O ye poor
Heart-weary toilers, come to this wide door
Of dear wood solitude, to wander free
And joyance take in their fair company.
Lo, where I lie here lapped in waters sweet
Of waveless indolence from head to feet,
How well I know the rapt ecstatic birth
Renewed without! the mirrored sky and earth,
Married in beauty, consonant in speech,
And uttering bliss responsive each to each.
The daintier beauty grows here at my door
In weed and brier; even through the floor
Springs, barbed on velvet, one bold raspberry,
Born for no fruitage, for no eye to see
But mine, in this my tented privacy.
How the ferns waver, wakened by no wind
Save the green flickering of their blossomy mind!
And there beyond, the water laps the land,
Encircling her with charm of silver sand,
The ring through which her beauty may not pass,—
No, not for mirroring in that still glass.

16

Now while the body lies supine in sound
And bathed by sovereign air from dewy ground,
Or winds who sweep untired through the night
Conserving balm of blessedness in flight,
Out fleets the soul, and takes her softly forth
To meet the dawn ; and whether south or north
Or east or west, some altar, bright with fire,
Springs up bedecked before her one desire
To sing her matins ere the daunting day.
The ashy dust of night falls swift away
From her strong pinions, and she rideth free
Serene upon the morning's majesty.
Above spice-budded tops of fringing firs,
The shimmering birches, delicate ministers
To eye's delight, and o'er the deepening rose
Of the still lake, a soundless shade she goes.
What shall withstand her ? Not the mountain wall
Where the first potencies of dawning fall,
Touching and moulding till awakes a flower,
A jewelled heart of light, a throne of power.
Not all the barriers of rock and stream ;
For who hath caught the swift, evanished gleam
Of Beauty's mantle hath the charmèd eye
Fated to follow wheresoe'er she fly.
O happy soul ! led only by the voice
That bids her turn to some more wondrous
    choice !
Upon the herby field she sets her foot ;
Staying, she listens there to creeping root ;
Blesses the opening bud, and smells the mould,
Sinks in a fern-bed where faint coils, unrolled,

17

Etch on the air a curving tracery
None but the morning's postulant may see.
She steals great gospels from a sphere of dew,
That little globe where ancient lore lies new ;
And while her tenderest fibres wake and stir,
The realm o'er which she reigns reconquers her.
Prostrate she falls in worship high and lone ;
She swoons with rapture by the altar-stone.
God and the world, — they are the dual Great,
And through her dust are they communicate.

RED MAGIC

I SOLD myself to the fearsome things in the
wood ;
And now am I fled from their bitter cherishing.
I gave myself for a drop of the thickened blood
That dabbles and drips on the innocent emerald
ring
Round the rotting branch where the owl sits dim
in the dark
And hoots, for the winds to hark.

I thought the blood of the wood was the red of life,
And if one of the fearsome things should but make
it flow,
A touch would stir up my soul into fiery strife,
And rapture enwrap it, and I should speed me
and go
To sail in the feathery air, and dart and leap
Where pools in the shadow sleep.

18

And now have I risen alone from that sullen hour, *Red*
And crawled forth into the sun where it used to fall ; *Magic.*
Darkened and dumb, I feel about for the flower
That yesterday bloomed alive. But I dare not call,
Lest the fearsome things should troop and gather
  again,
To shriek at my mask of pain.

MIST

FLEETING across the flood
Of the glimmering lake to the wood,
Look how it wavers and gleams, —
Diaphanous vesture of dreams !

WHEN DAYS ARE LONG

OH, time is so short, so short !
How would wise thrift employ it ?
Oh, the hoard of the hour is so small !
How shall man and a maiden enjoy it ?
Sweetheart, by flinging an arm
Round the neck of the summer weather ;
On the longest road under smilingest sky,
Footing it gayly together.

REVELATION

DOWN in the meadow, sprent with dew,
I saw the Very God
Look from a flower's limpid blue,
Child of a starveling sod.

THE HEART AND LOVE

(An Echo.)

COME into my garden-ground, O thou sweet
    of my soul, come in !
In the glamour and dusk of the dawn, ere the long
    bright hours begin,
While the flowers are still in their sleep, though
    all their breath is astir
With fragrance far-reaching yet faint, like the
    spirit of musk and of myrrh.
Come in, yea, and look thou alone on the dawn-
    flowers blossoming.
Come, bathe thee in purpling mists, while the
    rhythmical censers swing,
And listen, while songs more sweet than the heart
    of man can devise —
Ay, the very spirit of all the songs — like an
    angel choir shall rise.
Oh, what can I promise thee, love, in my garden
    far and lone,
When the sounds of the night are still, and the
    flower-sweet breeze hath flown ?
In my garden lone and far, curved over by fading
    skies,
Till only the stars know well where the bower
    of its beauty lies !
For thee, for thee was it sown in the spring of
    the heart's desire,
Sown in earth grown black and rich under touch of
    the master fire ;   20

For thee was its bosom stirred by a thousand seeds
 concealed,
Germinant growth of the under-world, the riotous
 weft and yield
Of a royal will and a fortunate day and the swing
 of a lavish hand.
Oh, come and reign over it, lord of the rose which
 is lord of my waiting land !
Sown for thee, loveliest ! yet in the sowing was
 never a thought of thee ;
For ever the lips of the gods are shut under mask
 of their mystery,
And ever the reason of travailing birth and the
 portent of days to be
Are hid in the leaves of the timeless book that
 only the One may see, —
The One unknown and yet knowing all, Who said
 when the years were new :
" Let the bud of delight in a garden grow, and
 be sprent with the mystical dew.
Let it take full joy of the wanderer wind, let it lie
 under bountiful rain,
And respond to the touch of the ministrant sun,
 in a passion of fervor and pain.
Let one only, the master of beauty, return, in
 response to the challenging cry :
'Come into my garden-ground, O love, for the
 soul of the dust am I ! ' "

LIFE

THE shadow on a sunlit leaf,
  By other leaflets laid thereon :
O fickle shade, so fair, so brief !
For with the sun — thou 'rt gone.

PAGAN PRAYERS

YOU that hold the world,
  Uphold me.
You that light the sun,
Make me see.
Bear with me my sorrow ;
Help me meet the morrow,
Patiently.

O'er road we may know not
To end we must fear not,
Guide us, O Mighty One !
March with us, heroes !

                           .

YESTERDAY

TO remember the tender foreknowledge of
    morn, at the even,
To yearn for the treasures desired upon earth,
  when in heaven,

Were as easy as seeking to joy in love-bliss and
   love-token
When a ripple has passed and the face of the dream
   has been broken.

NO ANSWER

WHAT does it mean when love grows cold?
    That morning dreams of youth were sold
For barter baser yet than gold?
That God Himself is waxing old?
Nay, ask me rather whence we draw our human
   breath,
Or what is death.

AN INVOCATION

O MELODY! O Melody!
   For whom the Muses sing and sigh,
And bind their loves in choric call,
Till all Olympus lies in thrall;
Oh, hither fly, and wait thou nigh
While our dull discords vainly die!

O siren old, in witching old,
Take up again thy harp of gold,
And strike the strings in moving strain
With echoing fall and soft refrain;
Then loud and bold the measure hold
Till some new tale is nobly told.

Yet if thou fear these valleys drear,
Our sullied springs and pastures sear,
Lend from above one lyric note
To pierce and rend our hollow rote ;
That we who hear with tunèd ear,
May dream we wake and thou art near.

THE RETURN

THE night was clear, without a star,
  For that the moon usurped the sky.
Dream-ridden surges moaned in sleep ;
The trees were still, nor sighed reply.
Without a sound I flitted forth ;
I knew my element, the air,
And all the swift intelligence
Create to flash and darkle there.

The faintest sun was not too far
To mark the track foreknowledge led.
My limbs were light as vapor blown;
At last I lived in being dead.
Though star-dust sowed the vault of time,
Soul-dust was I, and not afraid ;
A thousand suns might wheel and flash,
But course like mine need not be stayed.

On, on, I fled o'er windless wastes,
Heeding no longer day nor night.
I heard the singing of the spheres,
Their rhythmic roll attuned my flight.

24

I hovered over sombre voids ;
And when a star dropped into space,
I fell with it, but yet more swift,
Rapt winner of a timeless race.

Through hail I flashed and smothering sleet,
To bathe me in a flaming sun,
As 't were the milk of Paradise :
But all unspent, my bliss had done.
A thought, a breath ; I was recalled,
To speed unswerving to the door
Where joy was wont to stay my feet,
But where their tread would sound no more.

Alas ! the garden bloomed the same,
Though not one rose had ruth for me ;
Sorrow lay not on any bush,
Nor stirred the leaf of lightest tree.
The house lay wrapped in decent gloom,
An odorous darkness vainly sweet,
Where one sat watching by the bed,
Her tears fast falling o'er my feet,

And one stood weeping by its head.
But one in silence sat apart.
She did not hear my joyous hail ;
I heard the beating of her heart.
" Love ! love ! " I cried, " rejoice with me ! "
But still her dry lips would not move.
I kissed her sudden on the mouth.
I knew no word but " Love ! " and " Love ! "

25

The Return. All night we watched together there ;
Strange tryst we kept, my love and I !
My hurrying heart was hot with words
To teach her what it is to die.
Yet, barred within her beauty's cell,
She might not hear, she might not see ;
I was alive, but not to her,
And all her soul lay dead to me.

Ah, but the end is yet to read !
When the door opens at her plaint,
When she hath set one forward step,
With bliss foredone, with languor faint, —
Closer than dreams of me have been,
More dear than her immortal breath,
My breast shall be her porch of heaven,
My face her visioning of death.

FOREWARNED

PSYCHE hath found her Cupid out :
And wilt thou find out me ?
Then keep high heart and courage stout,
For thou 'lt not see me ringed about
With Cupid's bravery.

The god's true splendor, though unguessed,
Would well illume the night ;
But foolish Psyche might not rest
Till it should also bear the test
Of baser candle-light.

Thou art not Psyche, dearest maid?
Nor I the god of love.
Read, then, the riddle unafraid:
But let thy questing heart be stayed,
Nor seek her bliss to prove.

Give me the universe to roam,
The sky for breathing-space,
And though my will were thistle-foam,
No breeze but yet would blow me home
To thine adored embrace.

But if thou, loving, prove the spy,
Alas! what wilt thou see?
Flaws fitted to affright the eye
In one who still hath wings to fly,
Heart-wounded, and yet — free!

A WEST-COUNTRY LOVER

THEN, lady, at last thou art sick of my
sighing.
Good-bye!
So long as I sue, thou wilt still be denying?
Good-bye!
Ah, well! shall I vow then to serve thee forever,
And swear no unkindness our kinship can sever?
Nay, nay, dear my lass! here's an end of
endeavor.
Good-bye!

27

A West-
Country
Lover.

Yet let no sweet ruth for my misery grieve thee.
Good-bye!
The man who has loved knows as well how to
leave thee.
Good-bye!
The gorse is enkindled, there's bloom on the
heather,
And love is my joy, but so too is fair weather;
I still ride abroad, though we ride not together.
Good-bye!

My horse is my mate; let the wind be my
master.
Good-bye!
Though Care may pursue, yet my hound follows
faster.
Good-bye!
The red deer's a-tremble in coverts unbroken.
He hears the hoof-thunder; he scents the death-
token.
Shall I mope at home, under vows never spoken?
Good-bye!

The brown earth's my book, and I ride forth to
read it.
Good-bye!
The stream runneth fast, but my will shall out-
speed it.
Good-bye!

I love thee, dear lass, but I hate the hag Sorrow. *A West-*
As sun follows rain, and to-night has its morrow, *Country*
So I'll taste of joy, though I steal, beg, or *Lover.*
  borrow!
Good-bye!

DESTINY

RICH in all beauties art thou, love,
  Save those wherein high souls delight.
My slavish sense, my shuddering will,
Contend o'er thee in scornful fight.

Ah, many a year I vainly sought
Love's nobler largess, joy or woe!
Now, sick and shamed, I bear his dart:
Like Baldur, slain with mistletoe.

LOVE DENIED

DIAN looked down from hovering height, and
    saw Endymion sleeping,
The viny shadows playing round, and o'er his
  forehead creeping:
Tendril displacing dewy curl, and curl succeed-
  ing leaf.
O lavishment of loveliness, that light should be so
  brief!

Creeping through sedge and thorny wild, her
darling to discover,
Almost afraid of her own shade, came the chaste
maiden-lover;
And when, equipped with hunter's craft, her
jealous gaze had found him,
Within the charm of her white arm she fain had
clipt and bound him.

"Oh," sighed she, in the lonesome joy of that
subduing rapture,
"That I might seal the eyes of Night, and his
fair beauties capture!
What were the wrong to smooth one curl his
radiant brow adorning?
Nay, if I pressed his mouth to mine, were 't meet
for Juno's scorning?"

Ah! at the word, her cheeks were dyed, a pretty
redness turning;
She smote her brow, in sweet despite, to find it,
too, was burning.
And then, so cruelly and hard did her pure
thoughts deride her,
She blushed again, until it seemed the Morn
walked there beside her.

"Love-tokens pale," she murmured low, "when
love's not of the spirit;
And who would snatch at body's joy, a base thing
doth inherit!"

30

With that, her passion cold at heart, she fled to
upper ether,
And left Endymion sleeping on, the Dark and he
together.

ON PILGRIMAGE

(A.D 1250.)

MY love hath turned her to another mate.
(O grief too strange for tears!)
So must I make the barren earth my home;
So do I still on feeble questing roam,
An outcast from mine own unfriending gate,
Through the wan years.

My love hath rid her of my patient heart.
(Wake not, O frozen breast!)
Yet still there's one to pour her oil and wine,
And all life's banquet counteth most divine.
O Thou, Who also hadst in joy no part,
Give me Thy rest!

What strength have I to cleanse Thy stolen tomb,
For Christendom's release?
Naked, at last, of hope and trust am I,
Too weak to sue for human charity.
A beggar to Thy holy shrine I come.
Grant me but peace!

MAGDALEN

MINE eyes are shut, their fringes hid
Beneath the night's black coverlid.
No fiery, swift proclaiming spark
Pursues thy flight across the dark.

Yet if their burning sear thee still,
'T is God's high justice, not my will.
If He avenge my wrong and shame,
Am I to blame?   Am I to blame?

A FAREWELL

THOU wilt not look on me?
Ah, well! the world is wide;
The rivers still are rolling free,
Song and the sword abide;
And who sets forth to sail the sea
Shall follow with the tide.

Thrall of my darkling day,
I vassalage fulfil:
Seeking the myrtle and the bay,
(They thrive when hearts are chill!)
The straitness of the narrowing way,
The house where all is still.

TO CIRCE

NO, Lady, I 'll not sup with thee,
Lest bread should be denied.
I 'll sit down here beside my barren hearth,
And feed on pride.

Thy wine makes merry company ;
But freed from hilding fears,
I better love the honorable salt
Of mine own tears.

Yet the bright beaming of thy look
Might still my heart unbar,
If through this rifted thatch there had not gleamed
One cold, clear star.

RENEWAL

THOU, whose short path lay one with mine,
Did not our days fleet, velvet-shod ?
We proved the stars, and probed the deep ;
We wondered o'er the One called God.
It seemed discourse could have no end,
So sweet it was to find a friend.

Now, lacking thee, I lack delight,
While hours go crawling, fretting by.
Thought cries in vain, and grieving, finds
No kindly voice to give reply.

Renewal. To meet, touch hands, and part again,
Was joy's one drop in seas of pain.

Thou shallow Self, thy wailings set
    In minor key to mournful tune!
Roses still blossom, though they fade,
    And every year renews her June.
On Nature's page is graven deep,
" To have and love is not to keep."

But not to lose.   O day, be swift,
    When, wandering with joyous feet
Through worlds where dreams come warm to life,
    In some fair garden we may meet!
And " Thou ? " will one, all gladness, cry :
The other, well contented, " I ! "

THE MESSAGE

THROUGH the silence and midnight of
        life
Thy soul to my soul I heard calling,
In bugle-notes, golden and long,
In pearl-drops of melody falling.
Then in joy I rose up from my rest;
My heart stilled its beating to hear thee.
With swiftness I sandalled my feet
That quivered with haste to be near thee.

34

Thy message cleft night like a star.
"Seek thou," it sang, "desolate places.
Go whisper in hungering ears
And smile upon death-darkened faces.
I am thine, thou art mine," cried thy soul,
" Yet heed me, and pause not nor wonder
If God set our faces apart,
And hold us a lifetime asunder."

Then my heart rose in altar-flames high ;
It thrilled with the whiteness of burning.
My breath was the incense of prayer,
Heavy-sweet with pure passion and yearning.
" Thou art mine, I am thine," cried my soul,
" Then thus do I hold and I heed thee :
It is more to obey thy decree
Than lament lest I lack or I need thee."

The pathway appointed I tread,
Unheedful of pain or of pleasure ;
Yet still with thy step I keep time,
And God Himself marks us the measure.
Thy face fronts the dawn, mine the west ;
But farthest, we still are the nighest :
For souls are but married anew
When wedded alone to the Highest.

FAMINE

AT last she learns that love can die;
That ashes bank the grave of fire
Enkindled from the living sun,
To make her faith a funeral pyre.

White wonder clothes her stony glance;
She shudders that Eternal Right
Could so betray a seed to birth,
And let it die for lack of light.

Like one avowed the bride of death,
Unmurmuring, she sits apart :
Veiling, with snow of patient looks,
The unfed hunger of the heart.

ON THE FIELD

YES, that last blow struck through
Corselet and chain and all ;
Where pain's hot lightning flew,
Now the red droppings fall.

You the cold heavens send
In the hour of my thirsty need —
Help me, O soldier-friend,
To cover how I bleed !

EDWIN BOOTH

" Ay, every inch a king!"

NOW is the night, foreshadowed of our fears ;
The curtain falls, the lights fade, one by
one.
Darkness and silence from the widowed stage
Proclaim the great and final act is done.
Vain are the thundered plaudits of the house,
The laurel wreath, the players' loud acclaim ;
Thou art grown dumb to clamoring for response,
· Deaf to the ringing of thy jewelled name.
Thy crystal soul hath traversed back the pathway
whence it came.

They who the virtues of the mighty dead
Enwrap in majesty of broidered verse,
Call upon Nature, in her solitude,
His beauties and her sorrow to rehearse.
The forest and the field, the fitful wind
They challenge, and the ever-sounding wave,
To seek his spirit in the vast afar,
And drop their dews on his enrichèd grave,
Crowning the poet's lyric woe with some for-
lorner stave.

Greater than all the universe of space
The mimic world thou didst thyself create :
The subtile sphere, compact of passion's breath,
Where Nature bade thee hold imperial state!

37

There shall the mourning garments be outworn;
There shall the desolate their dirges sing;
No princeling may ascend the vacant throne,
Laying new triumph's gall to sorrow's sting.
"The King is dead!" we cry, but nevermore,
 " Long live the King!"

Of all the stops of mortal harmony
Master thou art forever, though in death.
The melancholy of the Dane is thine,
The poisonous blighting of Iago's breath.
Thou didst take on foul Richard's humpbacked
 soul,
And clasp it close, yet do thine own no wrong:
As 't were the mantle of Sir Caradoc,
Unerring witness sung in ancient song,
Destined to prove the pure of heart more pure,
 the strong more strong.

Slave of self-conjured evil, Cawdor's thane!
The jester, bitter-hearted, striking home!
The fox-robed cardinal, creating France,
And launching forth the curse of sovereign
 Rome!
Gallant Don César, lord of ragged lace!
These wert thou in their turn, and sorrow-blind,
Alas! thou wert the doited father, too,
Pelted by heaven, and stabbed by human kind:
Heartbreakingly confest, " I am not in my perfect
 mind!"

Such was thy Protean form, but what wert thou? *Edwin*
Booth.
A changing cloud, content to borrow hue
From lordly sun-rays that o'errule it quite,
And thus with color and with form endue?
Nay, rather let the time's remembrancing,
When it doth con anew thy mortal span,
Ignore thine art, if such despite may be,
But bow in awe before thy nature's plan,
Crying with trumpet tone, to alien ears, "This
    was a man!"

Thine was the guilt of filching heavenly fire;
Wherefore Jove's eagle fed upon thy heart.
Yet never word nor strangled cry betrayed
Responsive agony beneath the smart.
A thousand hovering spectres menaced thee   .
Bound, by eternal fiat, on the rock
Of mortal languishment: yet unappalled
As gallant bird beneath the tempest shock;
For still thy soul soared free, thy silence met each
    hideous mock.

And can such glory pass? Nay, thus thou art,
Where'er in world diviner thou dost walk,
Mated with love celestial, that doth spring,
Fragrant and fair, from life's divided stalk.
But we who knew thee may not cease to mourn
The moment's grief, the time's perpetual loss.
Not ours to pluck from thine engravèd name
Oblivion's cold and memory-choking moss:
Blest are we for so noble sake to bear affliction's
    cross.   39

Henceforward nevermore may Denmark's Prince
Pace through his tragic hour in sabled pride
But thou, the sceptre's rightful heir, wilt walk,
Eclipsing all his grandeur, by his side.
And dally as we may with pageantry
Wherein some newer actor plays a part,
The scene will fade, while thine enshadowed
form
Doth from the slumbrous aisles of memory
start, —
Again the lost but ever-reigning monarch of the
heart.

Farewell! farewell indeed! But take with thee
Our true allegiance to that orient land, —
The laurels and the rosemary of life
Lying unnoted in thy nerveless hand.
Take with thee, too, our bond of gratitude,
That in a cynic and a tattling age
Thou didst consent to write, in missal script,
Thy name on the poor players' slandered page,
And teach the lords of empty birth a king may
walk the stage.

HORA CHRISTI

SWEET is the time for joyous folk
Of gifts and minstrelsy;
Yet I, O lowly-hearted One,
Crave but Thy company.

40

On lonesome road, beset with dread,
  My questing lies afar.
I have no light, save in the east
  The gleaming of Thy star.

In cloistered aisles they keep to-day
  Thy feast, O living Lord!
With pomp of banner, pride of song,
  And stately sounding word.
Mute stand the kings of power and place,
  While priests of holy mind
Dispense Thy blessed heritage
  Of peace to all mankind.

I know a spot where budless twigs
  Are bare above the snow,
And where sweet winter-loving birds
  Flit softly to and fro;
There with the sun for altar-fire,
  The earth for kneeling-place,
The gentle air for chorister,
  Will I adore Thy face.

Loud, underneath the great blue sky,
  My heart shall pæan sing,
The gold and myrrh of meekest love
  Mine only offering.
Bliss of Thy birth shall quicken me;
  And for Thy pain and dole
Tears are but vain, so I will keep
  The silence of the soul.

41

IN EXTREMIS

NOT from the pestilence and storm —
  Fate's creeping brood, — the crouching form
Of dread disease, and image dire
Of wrack and loss, of flood and fire;
Not from the poisoned fangs of hate,
Or death-worm born to be my mate,
But from the fear that such things be,
        O Lord, deliver me!

Fear dogs the shadow at my side;
Fear doth my wingless soul bestride.
In the lone stillness of the night
His whisper doth mine ear affright;
His formless shape mine eye appalls;
Under his touch my body crawls.
Now, from his loathsome mastery,
        O Lord, deliver me!

I would not loose me, if I might,
From touch, or sound, or taste, or sight
Of all life's dread revealing.   Nay,
Were I God's angel, I would stay
Here on this clod of crucial grief,
And learn my rede without relief;
But from this basest empery
        And last, I would be free.

My fiend hath poisoned even the cup
Of faith and love. I may not sup
But horror grins within the bowl,
And spectre guests affright my soul.
Yea, and the awful Sisters Three,
Spinning the web eternity,
Have lost their solemn state, and wear
      The Furies' snakebound hair.

Out of the jaws of hell and night,
Lead my sick soul, O Sovereign Light!
Let me tread shivering through the cold,
Despised, forsaken, hunted, old,
Unloved, unwept, beneath the ban
Of sharpest anguish laid on man ; —
But from the monster foul I flee,
      O God, deliver me!

KNIGHTHOOD ETERNAL

DELAY no more by altar-fires, nor stay for
    prayer and vow !
The battle-ground 's beneath thy feet, the time for
    steel is now.
What need hast thou of mortal lance, of sword or
    saving shield ?
What need of armor burnished bright, by alien
    hands annealed ?

43

From helm to greave, thy mail shall be with thine
   own passion wrought ;
Tempered with heat of white desire, and forged by
   clanging thought.
Thy sword shall be the naked truth, for scabbard
   never made ;
Thy shield of holy chastity, twin foe of hacking
   blade.

The bowers of peace are cool and fair, but not for
   thee they bloom ;
What wouldst thou earn, O lingerer in rose-
   enshadowed gloom ?
One little hour of joyance vile, of base, self-tainted
   breath ;
Apples with ashes at the core, the cup that tastes
   of death.

The bugle cries for thee !   Arise, and face the
   bannered field, —
Vowed evermore to fight and die, but not to live
   and yield ;
Content to leave the day unwon, the lust of fame
   forego,
So thou mayst march one step in time, or strike
   one gallant blow.

HEIMGEGANGEN

WHAT word, O my daughter, what word
from the damp and the dark?
I put down mine ear to the grasses that brighten
thy roof-tree.
Speak thou, while I hark.

Good cheer, O my mother! such quiet and com-
forting cheer.
I sit here all day and I spin, in my little dark
corner.
My mother, dost hear?

I hear, O my daughter! but how can my heart
understand?
You speak not of stars and of prophesied rapture
and glories,
Of new sky and land.

Nay, nay, O my mother! how should I? for I
· am alone,
Spinning my thread in the dusk of this one little
corner,
Marked out for mine own.

I dream of the sky and the star-beams, of infinite
space;
Then house me in peace — yea, in peace! — in
my little dark corner:
I have gone to my place.

SLEEP

WITHDRAW thee, soul, from strife.
  Enter thine unseen bark,
    And sail across the dark,
  The silent sea of life.
Leave Care and Grief, feared now no more,
To wave and beckon from the shore.

  Thy tenement is bare.
    Shut are the burning eyes,
    Ears deaf against surprise,
  Limbs in a posture fair.
The body sleeps, unheeding thee,
And thou, my sailing soul, art free.

  Rouse not to choose thy way ;
    To make it long or short,
    Or seek some golden port
  In haste, ere springs the day.
Desire is naught, and effort vain :
Here he who seeks shall ne'er attain.

  Dream-winged, thy boat may drift
    Where lands lie warm in light ;
    Or sail, with silent flight,
  Oblivion cleaving swift.
Still, dusk or dawning, art thou blest,
O Fortune's darling, dowered with rest !

46

LETHE

YOU hope we shall remember, dear,
The happy days when we lived here?
Ah, child, what shouldst thou know of fear,
Whose soul is like a rosy leaf
Floating adown the stream of grief,
The velvet edge incurved, a boat
Unwet with woe, and made to float
Forgetful of the flood beneath,
Whose oozy waters smell of death!
Turn here thy gaze, and look on her,
Thy grandame, who wots not to stir
From her dull corner; note her face
With wrinkles lined; seek out the grace
That once adorned her heyday bloom,
Rusted and worthless in that tomb.
And think you she would greatly care,
If God should make her smooth and fair,
And round and rosy, eyes alight
With youthful pride and longing bright,
To keep that record of the years,
And trace those channels made by tears?
Saying: "In this I wept my son;
This came when old distrust begun;
That line was cut, O cruel spite!
When sweets of loving took their flight."

Nay, then, I think she'd find it good
To stand up in the lustihood

Of youthful grace and new-sprung pride,
And throw her worn-out flesh aside.
And so shall we, if in the day
When sins and ails are purged away,
The cunning record of the brain,
The hates and madness, grief and pain,
The murderous deed we did our friend,
The scoff for which there 's no amend
May die a natural death, and we
Again like little children be;
And caring not to understand
Our birth into that other land,
Roam through its valleys, hand in hand.

THE SILENT WATCH

FULL armed I fought the Paynim foe;
    Now palm to palm I lie,
My bed of stone, my covering
    The minster's vaulted sky.

Pilgrim and priest, move softly here,
    On vain or holy quest.
Let me sleep on, and take the meed
    Of my appointed rest.

Let me sleep on, until my soul
    Hath made her strong again
To fight the fight of good with ill,
    Of peace with mortal pain.

For one day there shall come a voice
  Sounding from sky to sea :
" Arise, Sir Knight, before My face !
  Now have I need of thee."

TRILBY

O LIVING image of eternal Youth !
  Wrought with such large simplicity of truth
That, now the pattern 's made and on the shelf,
Each vows he might have cut it for himself ;
Nor marvels that we sang of empty days,
Of rank-grown laurel and unprunèd bays,
While yet, in all this lonely Crusoe land,
The Trilby footprint had not touched the sand.
Here 's a new carelessness of Titan play.
Here 's Ariel's witchery to lead the way
In such sweet artifice of dainty wit
That men shall die with imitating it.
Now every man's old grief turns in its bed,
And bleeds a drop or two, divinely red ;
Fair baby joys do rouse them, one by one,
Dancing a lightsome round, though love be done ;
And Memory takes off her frontlet dim
To bind a bit of tinsel round the rim.
Dreams come to life, and faint foreshadowings
Flutter anear us on reluctant wings.
But not one pang, nay, though 't were gall of bliss,
And not one such awakening would we miss.
O comrades, here 's true stuff ! ours to adore,
And swear we 'll carve our cherry-stones no more.

DREAMS: RUBINSTEIN'S DANCE OF THE BAYADÈRES

O H for the tinkle of castanets !
The castanets!
When the twinkle of myriad lanterns frets
The languorous air, and over the tents
The lantern stars are burningly bent.
Chink ! Chink ! Chinkachink !
See every link
Of my burnished bangles beat and glance
Over my wrist where the pulses dance !

So, whirling and whirling and evermore twirling,
Still tracing the track of the sand-shower in swirl-
    ing,
When the wind of the desert is minded to beat
The earth into rings under rhythmical feet, —
All my hurrying soul sings in rhyme,
And the body's blood marks me the time.

And first the heads nod, —
For a Sultan 's a god ;
And a Vizier, my word !
He 's a lord.
See the smoke of their dozing upcurl !
See them watch the poor girl
Unwinding the smoke from its fold upon fold,
Silent they, and so cold !

But look ! now the twinkling and footing are faster,
Oh, faster and faster !
The body sways lower, it rests on the air.
(Ah, fair ! but a maiden is fair !)
The air's made of feathers from down of the dove,
And the arms bent above
Are the arching of Allah's great dome on the sky,
Still calling the pulses to fly
Ever fast and more fast,
Ere the moment be past.
Then the Sultan gives over his solemn puff-puff;
And as to the Vizier, why, he's had enough
Of tobacco, and wine, and the solace of sweets.
And now, while the music advances, retreats,
Quite into the mystical ring they go,
And dance like dervishes to and fro.
And up and down, and round and about,
Like Father Time in the Devil's rout,
With beard, and hand, and foot and glance,
The Sultan and Vizier are one with the dance.
Ah, well, my maidens, we're something worth,
So, sceptreless, swaying a lord of the earth !
Hush ! listen ! the music's falling, falling !
What is't I hear calling,
Over the reaches of wind-blown plain,
The grave-sown plain ?
(O love from the desert, O dawn of my day,
Slow, slower, ride slower, I pray,
That the dream may go on
Till the terrible truth-telling dawn,
On and on !)

51

Dreams. So comes he, with thunder of galloping feet,
And so am I fleet
To fly like a bird to his stirrup, his knee,
The cup of his welcome to be !

  . . . .

God ! the east is blood-red,
And the Sultan is lifting his head.
Shall I smother his yawns with a scream,
And tell him my dream ?

THE POET

BEAUTY enwrapt him like the cell
A flower-cup folds about the bee ;
And, leaning o'er her honeyed well,
He drank Eternity.

Then ere his housing felt decay,
Untired, he sought the outer light :
Winging the soul's unfettered way
In fragrance-laden flight.

THE SLANDERER

THE angels of the living God,
Marked, from of old, with mystic name,
O'erveil their vision, lest they see
One sinner prostrate in his shame.

52

And God Himself, the only Great,
    Preserves in heaven one holy spot,
Where, swept by purifying flame,
    Transgression is remembered not.

Yet thou, O banqueter on worms,
    Who wilt not let corruption pass! —
Dost search out mildew, mould, and stain,
    Beneath a magnifying-glass.

If one lies wounded, there art thou,
    To prick him deeper where he bleeds;
Thy brain, a palimpsest of crime,
    Thy tongue, the trump of evil deeds.

SEAWARD BOUND

GIVE me, in this inconstant ebb and flow,
    Some fixèd spot
Where I may plant the soul's desire, and know
    It withers not.

An argosy, swift under purple sail,
    Down sweeps the dawn,
Unloading all her spices to the gale,
    And is withdrawn ;

Yet no more sudden than the jewelled tower
    And front of day
Falls noiseless, gem from gem, at twilight's hour,
    And floats away.

Even that solemn star, the beacon blaze
    On reefs of night,
Wanes to a close when most the shipwrecked gaze
    Implores her light.

Love hath his funeral rites at Fancy's tomb;
    And Friendship's gate
Swings from within, to exiles making room
    For newer state.

O Thou, the Author of this whirling world,
    Create for me
Some sea of being where still sails are furled
    Eternally !

Or in that houseless mote, my drifting heart,
    Raise Thou a throne :
Spread silence round Thee, and dwell there apart,
    Awful, alone.

TEWKESBURY ABBEY

A SORDID town, scarred with one ruthless way,
Where thin-lipped houses mutter, each to each :
A squalid folk, delighting to betray
And jeer the pilgrim, though he speak their speech :
Dull, dusty stage, whereon the lust of power
Spread once a carpet spun from brothers' blood,
And squandered there that little precious hour
God granted men to buy eternal good.
Ah, but in forest aisles there smileth peace,
Though the clouds crack above that cloistered calm ;
And 'neath this vaulting doth contention cease,
And Memory heal herself with Beauty's balm.
Now Margaret, the Lion-Heart, may trust
Her hunted Prince with Clarence, dust to dust.

CONTENT

O TIME, thou niggard, thievish almoner,
Doling thy scanty gold to snatch it straight !
No longer may I stay to supplicate,
Though for the coin which buys me blissful myrrh
And frankincense of knowledge, fee to her,
The Sibyl Art, that even now so late
She might admit me at her mystic gate,
And unto me perfection minister.
Not all thy wealth might stead me ; yet I know
Now at the last where Light Eternal lies :

Content. There on the green of forest architraves,
The deepening of the sun's forgotten glow,
The elusive spirit locked in Beauty's eyes,
The thunder of apocalyptic waves.

THE HEART'S TRUE CHOICE

SHALL I condemn thee to the barren hills
And dreary vales of my life's heritage,
Saying, " Because I love thee, thou shalt wage
Perpetual feud with joy, nor shun those ills
That hover where my soul perforce fulfils
Her course of ancient doom, her pilgrimage
Of soiled intent, of weak, abandoned rage
For burnished deeds, of ever-clashing wills " ?
Nay, I would have thee led by fair device
To deep forgetfulness of grief and me.
Fain would I buy thee, at my sorrow's price,
Some happy isle, ringed round with smiling sea,
Where thou shouldst pluck pure flowers of Paradise,
And drink their fragrance everlastingly.

THE SPIRIT'S HOUR

" LET me be free from thee, belovèd dead ! "
So through the weary day aloud I cry,
Seeking, with strained and agonizing eye,
Thy shadow, trembling at my side ; thy tread

With hungry ear ; thine olden touch on head
Or lips, to give my devil, Doubt, the lie.
" Life claims me ; so do thou, in grace, deny
Such dreams, until I make the earth my bed ! "
Thus do I mourn by day ; but when the night
Lights, with her dusk, the all of mystery,
My spirit quickens till thy spirit bright
Enfloods it.   Short and sure the road to thee.
Earth to her heaven responds, and, vanquished
   quite,
I pray the silence, " Let me not be free ! "

MAN TO WOMAN

THOU art not mine nor shalt be !   This I
   know
While the prize glimmers in my happy hold ;
For though Love live till Memory hath grown
   old,
And lift his torch to light the way we go, —
Though, equal-spanned, our thoughts together flow
Like wedded rivers winding, fold on fold,
Undried in sun nor stayed by winter cold,
Thou art not mine, howe'er we vow it so.
Thy soul is but the glass wherein I see,
With blinded flash of rapt intelligence,
Riven ideals in new-born beauty laid
On the bright bosom of eternity ;
And learn, with prescience far outstripping sense,
The image mine, the mirror His Who made.

THE UNSEEN FELLOWSHIP

O YE mysterious ministrants of night !
Will ye be gone because the specious light
But seems to brighten o'er my spirit's dole ?
Ye who, untired, have tended my sick soul
With soft, slow touches, cooling as the stream
Delayed in strenuous course where rushes dream
Of frosty norlands or the tufted pine ;
Who, with warm whispers, airs incarnadine,
Suffused the pallor of this arid room
Till the rich husk of midnight's budded bloom
Broke in a marigold heaven of sunset grace,
And vaporous lightnings lovelily laid bare
Some all-divine, some long-desirèd face
(Moon-pale for shadowing of the aureoled hair)
Gleaming and bending o'er the bars of pain,
Pure as May mist, or rainbow after rain.

Ye came not at the spirit's first sharp call ;
But when of dulling death she most was fain,
Then did your wings awake this iron wall
(Chamber of care, dark cell of brooding Dis)
Into one pulsing reredos of bliss.
And your still counsel was the litany
Of acquiescent joy in pangs to be.

For ye do know !
Whether your feet, unled, our path have trod,
Or in illuminating whiteness go
Along the rapt, mysterious ways of God ;

Whether, in learning all, ye suffered sore,
Or be of those who serve Him evermore
From some fine trance of new-dissolvèd sleep,
Awaked by holy chrism, to sacrament
Of equal love and equal wisdom blent,
And forth, to do His bidding, joyous leap, —
Still do ye break with us our stony bread,
And share our bitter wine, in vigils dread.

Heralds of sacred silence are ye all,
Who, knowing many things, may nothing tell;
Who may not whisper : "This is ill" or "well,"
But only o'er the night's abysses call,
Plangent and clear, as though a new star shone,
"Soul, thou art not alone!"

Go not, O faithful! with the mounting sun
Mortality's tormenting hath not ceased ;
Nay, rather be her heavy toils increased,
For noon's sad, upland marge lies still unwon.
Walk with us, lest we pluck the flaunting flower
Of life's delight, to paint our garlands gay,
Forgetting gracious herbs, till that bleak hour
When day's great king hath reft his court away.
Walk with us! or if still supremely blest,
The dawning waft ye home, to bathe your wings
With dews unspent, or sink in brooding rest
Where some bird-throated cherub softly sings, —
Yet should the Night her holy fires inflame
To sear the soul anew, in one Great Name,
When we, in dross, upon that altar burn,
As He, your Lord, doth live, ye shall return.

THE FLIGHT OF THE FAIRIES

WHAT serves the earth for sleep
   Is but a dream-tower builded on a dream :
A brooding and a premonition deep
Of all that will be when the fresh-sprung stream
Of day's delight rolls outward from the sun,
Hailing a new world's wonder well begun.
Fuller of counsel than at glowing noon,
She lies full-bosomed to the sentient moon
(Unsatisfied allurer of the night)
And gives in beauty what she takes in light.
O constant, sweet quiescence of repose !
As if a pollen-rich, musk-hearted rose
Should seal her petals, in recurrent rest,
So to shut all her sweetness in her breast,
And swing there, of her self-communing fain,
Secure in knowing, " I shall be a rose again. "
One night there was, now many a night gone by,
When Cynthia set her broad shield in the sky,
Symbol of peace and plenteous content,
And dropped herself to earth. Where'er she
   went
The dew was frosty underneath her tread,
And all the boughs grew silver overhead,
Touched by a glory ye may never guess
Who have not viewed her nearer loveliness.
She might not stir without it. As when watery
   air
Cools into clouds a thousandfold more fair

Than still blue ether, so her amorous leaping
Bloomed in a charm ne'er breathed from Cynthia
    sleeping.
Her body's presence moved pure crystalline,
And even her radiant shadow seemed to shine.

In her forsaken hall, one iris cloud
Moved regnant in her place, with power en-
    dowed
To hew the underlying plain
In shape of hill and valley, and again
Loose his great fancy into piling waves
Of wind-stirred light; or blocking o'er those
    caves
Scooped out of blackness, where, in shadow drest,
Strange mammoth monsters lay in uncouth rest.
These beauties, wrought in Titan mood,
Were fit for sporting of some giant brood
Who take the earth for playmate, and in spite
At her dull gentleness, poor, patient wight!
Force her to mask and mime for one short night.
But such gigantic pageantry of change,
Through which her moonlight fantasy did range,
Were less than loveliness to those still spots
Quite overhung with leaves, the hidden grots
Where, bowered in crowding green,
Bedecked with coral set in mossy sheen,
And glittered round by grassy lances keen,
Still lordly Oberon the great,
Purest of fairy blood,
Doth hold his whimsy mood,

And keep his elfin state.
On this night breathed a sigh
From fringèd canopy
And wilding forest of the maidenhair.
The sigh rose into song,
Chanted with changing measure, and erelong
The song a chorus grew and filled the air,
One ecstasy of limpid melody.
" Here in the ferny brake
The firefly starts awake.
The glowworm, bold night-lover,
Moon secrets doth discover.
O follower of the night,
Lend me thy light !
Star of the oozy dark,
Give me thy spark !
Old killjoy owl o' the bough
On linden-tree,
Thy topaz eyes shall now
Our lanterns be !
Nay, never blink and blink,
Nor blinded slink
Back into covert !   Nay, come out,
For the moon 's about,
And we, the well-wishers, the lovers of all,
Hold thee and the forest in thrall.
Here all together
We 'll tweak the feather
That grows o'er thy topaz eyes.
Thou canst not flee to thy sheltering tree,
For we too can rise,

And our chariot flies,
With a wish, to the height
Of thy craven flight.
Warders we of the wood,
Lovers we of the flood,
Gay little workmen, whose doing
Is ever pursuing
Of fleet-footed pleasure
And balmy-breathed leisure.
Gnat-Sting and Bat-Wing,
Bloom-Button, Pollen-Ring,
Light o' the Hour,
Joyance in Flower,
Honey-Tub, Lily-Throat,
Bee-Belly, Robin's-Note!
Here we come by the dozens,
Brothers, gossips, and cousins.
We are the elves, the only
Lovers of all the lonely
Sweet hidden faces
Of far forest places."

Ah! then swept Cynthia forth from leafy cover,
And all the ground beneath her feet bloomed
    over
With frosty flowers sprung from that pure vine
Whose root is moonbeam, and whose leaf doth
    shine
Celestial white.   The maid glanced down at all
    this glory,
And stayed transfixed to read her footsteps' story.

Forward she bent, as in a rapturous dream ;
(So bowed Narcissus once above the stream ;
So beauty might her fairest charms discover
And wake to find herself her own best lover)
Then, like a nymph pursued, she straight looked
    back,
And o'er her shoulder gazed upon her track.
And ever where she looked was loveliness,
And ever did her light her beauty bless.
There as she paused, her limbs and radiant dress
Were painted on the leaves, celestial fair,
Whiter than silver clouds on crystal air. ·
Then sudden on she sped, as if the chase
Drew out her soul in one swift headlong race.
But not to kill the deer !   To conquer joy,
And chain the world into one night's employ.
They see her ! ay, they see ! the elfin band
Troop from the fern-grove, hand in dainty hand,
And in the shining of her mantle's shade,
Tread out their fairy ring ; then low obeisance paid
To her, the puissant ruler of the ample hour,
Break into song, the while her high-orbed power
Sinks into softness all were fain to see,
Lulled with emotion at their harmony.
Her look melts into love divinely tender ;
Lower she bows beneath her own surrender.
She stands pure maiden, stripped of high estate ;
They are so little, how should she stay great ?

So the fairies sing, and, singing,
Set the sylvan glade to ringing :

" We know thee for the one enwrapt in splendor
Who dost inhabit all the courts of night ;
We hail thee now, the guardian sweet and tender,
Whose fostering foot awakes the world to light.

" Ah ! we 're sick of rhyme and reason,
Tired are we of time and season.
This is no verse we made for thee.
We stole it, queen, from a bird in a tree.
Now we 're tired of dragging the linkèd chain
Of stiff-joint rhyme, by might and main.
Here 's a cobweb ! trip it, Cynthia !
Try it, dearest, best and fairest !
Singing 's but a heavy pleasure ;
Join us now, and tread a measure !
Worship sits on addled eggs.
All our loving 's in our legs."
And round and round they haled, the hoiden
    crew,
While Dian laughed till all the vale thrilled
    through ;
Then leaped she from their midst, and singing ran
Swifter than her own peace at foot of man.
Sweet baby hootings followed, while the elves
Rolled in the murky glade to still themselves ;
Tired of their tricking, sick of silly fun,
And half their nightly revels not begun.
But listen ! hark ! swift as the living spark
Launched from a torchlight through the dark,
One comes, the fairies' messenger,
And all the leaves with listening 'gin to stir.

Softer than silence his tuned whispering,
Richer than waft of rhythmic-waving wing.
" Hear me, O forest folk !
Form ye in mystic ring,
For the word of your king.
Omen hath threatened us,
Woe 's in the air !
We of the fairy brood
Sicken in doleful mood.
Woe 's in the air !
The fairy honor 's sold ;
Fairy hearts are cold ;
For Oberon the king,
Oberon grows old !
Ambition hath won him.
Mortal doings have undone him.
He hath meddled, mixed, and mated,
Till his fairy days are fated
Still like mortal hours to run,
And fail with every waning sun.
Yea, he hath built with mortals, and hath striven,
He for an empty gain, they for their heaven ;
Fought for them with main and might,
Made their silly wrong come right.
With their false ambition fired,
He hath striven and aspired
Somewhat like a man to grow, —
To love, to suffer, and to know.
He hath tried to lift it, the earth-burden,
And the earth-curse bears upon him wearily ;
No more wishing brings a joyous guerdon,

But he travails drearily.
He hath caught the man-disease, the mortal pining,
He hath drunk the cup of human pain;
Henceforth all his happiness entwining
In the root that springs to mortal bane.
Woe hath laid hand on him,
Blighting and bold.
Now Oberon grows old!"

Fear fell on the fairies.
With sibilant hushes,
The low wind came wailing
In gusts through the bushes.
Gray fate stalked upon them
Through deepening gloom;
The lot of their leader
Foreshadowed their doom.
"Where now shall we wander?"
Sprite called unto sprite.
"The sting of despair
Lies in olden delight.
Who now shall redeem us,
If Oberon fail us?
What might shall surround us,
If earth-doom assail us?
Now, in delight's employ,
Who shall plant seeds of joy,
Living henceforth to bless
Flowers of idleness?
Wood-gods defend us!
Dian befriend us!"

" Up with thee, fairies!
Flit o'er the bracken
Ere the bright heaven
Her dial may blacken.
Seek within bloom and bud ;
Float on the under flood ;
Waken the sleeping leaf ;
Read ye the ancient rune,
Potent and brief !
For this moment of danger
Was aforetime foretold ;
And the wood-gods have left us
Their counsel of old.
Silence your wailing tune !
Run for the fairy rune ! "
Stillness enwrapped the wood.   The fairy tread,
Fainter than raindrops, beat the mosses' bed.
One leaf another stirred, in counsel tender,
As when love turns to love, in sweet surrender.
A foredone petal fell, and kissed the earth,
So blessing her for fostering of birth,
And her long nourishing of bloom and breath.
Such stillness thrills with life, and knows not death :
The silence of a sleep entranced with dreams,
When still the topmost froth of joy but seems
To kiss the beaker of heart's full content.
So through the rapt wood mood the fairies went
Seeking, aye seeking out the hidden scroll
Create to save them from the plague of soul.

I know not, I, whether the quest attended
By such dumb fear with that one night was ended.

Some say the magic word was swiftly found
Deep in the bosom of that circling ground
Kept chaste and fair for elfin revelling.
Some say his dainty majesty, the king,
Came on it, by good chance, that very hour,
Lurking unguessed in all its mystic power
Within the network of a living leaf.
Some say 'twas seen on Cynthia's garment hem,
Wrought all in curious cipher, gem on gem.
Some say the fairies, wishing, wished it straight
By dim dream-porches through the ivory gate;
And there it bloomed before them rapturously,
A blossom they alone might touch and spy.
I know not; yet one watching, overbold,
That broidered pageant hath the secret told:
How all the fairies rustled to and fro,
Like busy leaves, till their one moment's woe
Changed, on a sudden, to a mad delight.
And how they spent the remnant of the night
With brewing purest broth, in heat of moon,
After the spell of that strange, mystic rune.
And how they straightway cried, with urgent voice,
Upon their king, bidding his soul rejoice;
For they had found the source of elves' delight:
A fusion meant to make black hair from white,
And supple joint from out the creaking hinge,
And thrills of joyance from old age's twinge.
And how the king himself came riding swift
On a light-beam that seemèd but a rift
Within the darkened air; and how they drank
Of their rich brew together, till down sank

69

The morning star; and then a shining way
Opened before them like the new-sprung day.
Straight from the earth it ran and pierced the sky,
There where the dawn hath set her minstrelsy.
And all the fairies fled that radiant road
To some ethereal and far abode
Prepared for them ere earth had grown too rude
For harboring of her most delicate brood.

Some say 't was Cynthia's hall they sought at last.
I know not; yet I saw her shield hung fast,
Nailed to the throbbing dome of heaven, last night,
And never did it shine more purely bright:
As if the maiden set it there to tell
Where beauty liveth, there may fancy dwell;
And no sweet dream within the heart hath root,
But lies a land wherein the dream bears fruit.